THE HAIRDO THAT GOT AWAY

Joseph Coelho   Fiona Lumbers

Andersen Press USA

Dad takes me to the barber's once a
month, without fail, come rain or shine.
I watch my hair fall into my lap
as the barber chats.

"Your hair is tangled like Samson, the super-strong, long-haired warrior who could do whatever he wanted. Your fringe is long like Rapunzel, the princess trapped in the tower."

Dad tells the barber to shave cool things
into the back of my head, and afterward
we joke and make up rhymes . . .

"It's an arrow to help you keep your head high!"

"Up to the sky."

"As you go around school . . . "

"I'm gonna look cool!"

But Mom thinks the arrow on my head is not right for school.

Without hair to cover my ears, I can hear everything.
So I get under my covers and imagine I'm alone in a
tower like Rapunzel or in a battle like Samson,
fighting yelling lions and shouting armies.

Days pass and my hair gets big, but come rain or shine,
Dad doesn't come to take me to the barber's.
The arrow has gone from my head.

Weeks pass and my hair gets huge, but come rain or shine,
Dad doesn't come to take me to the barber's.
I can't fit my hat on my head.

Months pass and my hair gets ginormous, but come rain or shine, Dad doesn't come to take me to the barber's.
There are knots inside my head.

My hair gets curly, wavy,
tangled down my back.

It's been two months, four days, and eight hours since I last saw Dad. I sit in my usual seat at school.

"Who's the new kid?"

"I've never seen him—her?—before."

My hair gets curly, wavy,
tangled down my back.

It's been two months, four days, and eight hours since I last
saw Dad. I sit in my usual seat at school.

"Who's the new kid?"

"I've never seen him—her?—before."

I am getting hot and bothered under all my hair.
Things have changed for me, and everyone knows it.
Even Miss Clarke doesn't recognize me . . .
"New child—come to the front and introduce yourself."
"But Miss, it's me."
"Pardon? I can't understand you under all that hair."

Tomorrow is the school trip to the zoo.
Normally I'd tell Dad and he'd
give me some money.
I collect erasers and keyrings
and buttons.

I need some spending
money to keep my
collection going.

It's been six months, eight days, and twelve hours since I last saw Dad, so I figure I better ask Mom.

But her hair is so long, she can't hear me.

I'm here at the stupid zoo with no pocket money,
so no erasers or buttons or keyrings for my collection.

If no one knows who I am, then I might as well
be like Samson and do whatever I want!

We go past the baby emus.
They squawk, they stare, they jump the
fence, they nest in my hair!

"Child, will you stop teasing the animals!" says Miss Clarke.

We pass the lions.
They whimper, they stare,
shaking their manes,
scared by my hair.

"Child, will
you STOP teasing the
animals!" shouts Miss Clarke.

We pass the buffalo.
They moo, they stare,
they bash at their pen,
they stampede everywhere.

"CHILD, WILL YOU STOP
TEASING THE ANIMALS!"
thunders Miss Clarke.

I'm in Mr. Burgess's office—he's the principal and he's bald.
We have to talk about my behavior at the zoo
while everyone else is at recess.

But he doesn't yell at me—instead he gives me
a book full of stories about people with lots of hair.

There's Rapunzel: her hair grew so long, a prince climbed up it. If my hair was as long as Rapunzel's, Dad might use it to climb up to our apartment.

And there's Samson: his hair gave him strength, but also got him in a whole lot of trouble—a bit like me.

After school I see Mom with a man covered in hair.
Curly, wavy, tangled hair down his back, over his ears,
over his eyes, long at the sides.

It's Dad!

His hair has been troublesome for him too.
His feelings got him hot and bothered and
tangled in frowns and knotted in sadness.

But all he wanted to do was come home,
and now he is back.

The three of us all get a new hairstyle.
I watch my hair fall into my lap and I feel strong like
Samson defeating an army and happy like Rapunzel
climbing down from her lonely tower.

The three of us laugh and joke
as I watch my hair fall into my lap . . .

Tangles of sadness—snipped to smiles.
Knots of worry—trimmed to tickles.
My family—woven together.

For the teachers, who know the power a
book recommendation can hold — J.C.

For Sean — F.L.

American edition published in 2019 by Andersen Press USA,
an imprint of Andersen Press Ltd.
www.andersenpressusa.com

First published in Great Britain in 2019 by Andersen Press Ltd.,
20 Vauxhall Bridge Road, London SW1V 2SA.

Text copyright © Joseph Coelho, 2019
Illustration copyright © Fiona Lumbers, 2019

Distributed in the United States and Canada by
Lerner Publishing Group, Inc.
241 First Avenue North
Minneapolis, MN 55401 USA
For reading levels and more information, look up this title at www.lernerbooks.com.

Printed and bound in China.

Library of Congress Cataloging-in-Publication Data Available
ISBN: 978-1-5415-7841-8
eBook ISBN: 978-1-5415-7842-5

1 -TOPPAN-5/1/19